THE TRAVELLER

---

the untold stories of Cupid

$$- \hbar -$$

CONSECUTION ONE
Utterance Twenty One of Twenty Two

KEN KAMMAL

THE TRAVELLER

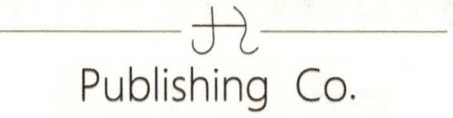

Publishing Co.

The Traveller: *the untold stories of Cupid -consecution one*
Utterance Twenty One of Twenty Two

For more information, email: contactus@thetravellerpublishing.com
The Traveller Publishing website: www.thetravellerpublishing.com

ISBN: 978-1-954734-01-2 (Paperback)
ISBN: 978-1-954734-04-3 (Hardcover)
ISBN: 978-1-954734-02-9 (e-book)

The Library of Congress Control Number (LCCN): 2021901830

Author's Note

This is a true story of my experiences, dreams, visions, writings, and paintings; it is necessary to note that we all have the gift to seek ourselves within. Therefore, I encourage you, in some medium, to share your soul's journey or your spirit's plight in this creation. It is one, I know will have its moments and experiences that can evolve you into the ultimate BEING you seek.

Acknowledgments

I would like to thank everyone and everything that has made this journey possible. Every experience and moment has granted me the ability to write this story of the SOUL. This is a Soul-biography and a testament to the intelligence, brilliance, courage, peace and radiance of LOVE, and the awareness of the Soul. And, as I travel this beautiful path, may I know no truth, but Truth beyond LOVE.

Dedication

I dedicate this Utterance to the ONE, and the One in all of us.

Table of Contents

Author's Note..i

Acknowledgments ii

Dedication iii

Utterance Twenty One of Twenty Two...1

Introduction 3

Utterance Twenty One of Twenty Two "The Newcomer"................5

Utterance Twenty One of Twenty Two

I am the Traveller. These are my accounts of the vast wellspring of journeys of many lives. Of the dreaming heart, generating, operating, and destroying worlds. And the utmost necessary beliefs, beauty, and hardships within these journeys. That is the reality of the Traveller, the untold stories of Cupid.

Introduction

REMEMBER NORTH, North-East, North-West, South-East and South-West. I will repeat, remember North, North-East, North-West, South-East and South-West! I laid there, back flat against the floor, looking up at the light at the top of what seemed to be the inside of some sort of tower. I looked up, noticing that each of the floors in this tower had doors going in a circular pattern around each floor. I was wondering what was on the floors, as well as what was behind the many doors.

A voice echoed in my head loudly, breaking my wonder of thought about this place. I tried to get up, but I laid there. The tower floor was dry, sparsely covered in sand. As I turned over to my side, the granules of sand and the cold floor were against my face and the side of my body.

I turned over to see this distorted image of a man leaning against the tower walls. With my clouded vision of him, I could see slightly that he was dressed in black. He stood there, saying to me, "Get up!" I tried to, but to no avail … I could not get up. "Get up, you know how to get up. Get up off the floor and stand!"

Then suddenly, right in front of me, laid a replica of me, as if I were looking in the mirror at myself. Lying there on the bottom floor, there was a stillness in the eyes and the body of this identical image of me. He just laid there, facing me unclothed. His facial features just like mine, not one flaw or imperfection; a copy of me. The vibration and sound of our heartbeats filled the space between us.

The sound of this double beating of hearts was only broken by the distorted image of that man confidently piercing at me from against the wall. This man kept yelling. His voice continued to echo in my head saying, "Now get up!" in a direct voice. "This time, not with your mind nor flesh reacting."

I thought about my intent, from my heart pushing and thrusting me up. I lifted up in a vampirine-revival like manner. I stood there, heart frantically beating. I could hear my very pulse beating within my ears.

Then suddenly I awoke, although barely awakened and not that coherent. I seemed to have fallen or been pulled back into my bed by gravity, as though I was seemingly shaking and levitating over my bed.

I dreamt of me being in that labyrinth tower, with floor after floor leading up to the center of the tower, in which a deep array of light beamed into it.

The daylight had come into the room of my residence and presented me with a calm and conflicting morning. The breeze from outside had blown into my little room, and the day seemed reasonable. There was not a sound or noise of nature, just silence.

As I emerged from my residence and went outside, the sunny skies were met on both sides with silvery charcoal-like clouds, forming a path. It was the divided skies that made my path.

I was trying to find myself in the misery and motives of an act they called life. Although these morning skies also presented this twilight, I found refuge in it. If it were not for the twilight skies that cooled my headway, I would not have sought to leave this life.

Utterance Twenty-One of Twenty-Two

"The Newcomer"

<u>The Tower and the Path</u>

THE TRAVELS had begun, the path split, and the skies showed the way. Lifetimes of sorrow and regret had parted; they had to be divided. And the sum of thought had equated through the quake of a utopia. Without finding themselves, some had thoughts of worldly desirables, and some were givers and takers of the same yoke. Some wore Love as an honor and some were convinced that Love was a mere feeling, emotion, or thought. Some had their own beliefs which they openly shared with the world, as a so-called gift from their God and Gods. Although their God and Gods were not the savior of anyone. They had no idea they were the awaited savior and prophesized angel to all, but most of all themselves.

I met an Angel that night; he was me. I was the jewel that he was waiting for, to awake. I was looking upon myself, looking upon myself. There was the Bow and Arrow of Love I had to find in the annals within the monolith of me.

The bow was made of spirit and flesh created from the mirroring of the soul. The bow was marked with lifetimes of egotism and the ego demurred and demonized. Like a tree, it even carried the rings of the years marked within its very make-up.

The battle of one's own self was a test of the bow's flexibility and fortitude, but nothing other than the will to Love would sharpen the Bow's preciseness and accuracy. It had to be precise of equal measure of strength in Love, and to never break or bend in Love's emotional rapture. For there was a war of soul and solace.

I walked for days as the skies brewed of a deep dark silvery sky on each side of the path that I followed in the sky. It was only upon the visions throughout the day that I placed a foot in front of another, hoping to find anything of meaning to follow in this land I traveled. And when I rested, the night sky casted itself upon the path, and my dreams took me to meet the tower's occupants.

I could not be more filled with the suffocating air that consumed my very being. My shoes I had worn were exposing my flesh, the bottoms tattered and worn. In my visions and dreams this same suffocating air was released from my Being. It was like a carriage, riding on a hot air balloon. There was an emptiness; I tried to pull from earth's gravity and earthly ways in my visions and dreams.

Observing myself; I looked upon this wondrous and beautiful path in front of me. So, I continued this life's path full of haste, love, excitement, gratitude, grace, posture, the premise of not knowing, and a healthy fear of the void of expectations. There is a perfectly good reason to have a fear of the void; it is a dark and empty place.

At least that is what I thought. Some think it is a place where so-called evil lurks, however, it is where you can create the most beautiful things. You can be made anew; it is the energy that is filled with the great light. The void or darkness is the place in which I had to seek to be me. To understand that the great journey is merely the great darkness and the light working in unison with me. I find it to be the great and beautiful divine whore.

I walked and walked through wide plains. One night, as I sat at the cusp of where the plains meet the wooded forest. I dreamt that my brow and my line of sight was just above the second-floor level of the tower in my previous dream. The tower was perfect in a circular design; every level, every square inch was smooth without a flaw, like the smoothness of the inside of a seashell. The light pierced through and illuminated all the floors from above. It was an intense light, as though I was staring into the sun.

Suddenly, the light swallowed my very environment, and I could hear from a distance the rails of a train track crackling. The background sound of the rails carried a tune of an amplified tuning fork, changing in vibration as the sound of the train seemed to come closer and closer.

Amid the forest, I was swept up in the swift movement of a train. Everything was dim and dark at first. Then, a flood of light came through the train car windows. I looked out the window with a view of an enormous desert. The desert valley was vivid and bright, and the train as well as its tracks seemed to cut right through it. While I was seated there, a woman with red hair appeared to me, and we engaged in eye contact.

She was beautifully stunning with an air of sophistication in my eyes. She delighted my senses with her indulging figure. I was in awe of her reddish hair. Her luxurious red hair blew gently with the winds that flowed throughout the train car. This red-haired woman looked at me as though I knew her. It was as though I was a familiar face to her.

She sat across from me inside the train, one row up from where I sat. As we glided through the valley, it was only us on the train, yet the train car seemed so full. I just sat back and marveled at her beauty, not saying a word for a while.

I was consumed with a sort of erotic awakening and an ever quickening in my heart, but I wanted to be subtle in my words. Not startle her or say anything that would make her resistant. In that moment, I shied away, but my connection with her was obvious to my soul, and my curiosity seemed to push me to talk to her.

She was a temptress, a feminine figure with the ability to invoke the easiness of oneself. She was a conspirator in the art of seduction and reasoning. She was a feminine being beyond measure. I would lose myself in her provocative and alluring gaze as well as her aura.

As the wheels rolled over the tracks, her red hair was blowing, as the beautiful light and warm breeze entered the compartment of the train. I asked her, "What is your name?" She replied, "It is…"

At first, I could not make out what she said her name was. I asked her again, and she replied, "Robyn." I thought to myself, what a fitting name for a woman with red hair. As we began to talk on the train, I could no longer hear the train tracks. Her hair shined a light that was like the bright light of the tower's ceiling in my dreams, and from there, this experience with Robyn vanished. But my dream was ongoing. I was on the second floor of the pristine tower.

All the doors were open. I was met at the entrance by a young man named Keymaster. Keymaster, so virile, such youth and full of vigor. You could feel it in his being as he approached me with the utmost regard.

I could see inside, behind the doors; it was a multitude of beautiful columns. Orange and reddish in color, perfectly smooth, calcified columns everywhere. The beautiful colors danced with the light that entered this room. I caressed the columns inside the circular room with my hands and my senses.

Keymaster told me he was a master of opening doors, gateways, vortexes and vertices; a very charming figure. He did not mince words. He was confident, and as a matter of fact, he was connected to this world that was supposedly a dream of mine. Was that not what I always sought, connecting with those unimaginable parts of life?

Unexpectedly, there was a sound of buzzards that brought me to, and I awoke in the middle of the forest kneeling, full of perspiration and exhausted, by a shallow creek. I drank the water with the effort of a man who had taken thousands upon thousands of steps over a sultry sun and a humid moon. It was a journey so far, that I even asked a nowhere God for his hand. Even that came back void, and how could it not?

I could see the depth of the creek, but I was so amazed by the beauty of my current visible world. I put my entire face underneath the water to cool my skin from that sultry sun. I took off my tattered and dingy shirt, rinsing the shirt in the cool waters of the creek. Cooling my neck with it like an ice pack over bruised flesh.

I drank from its waters for a while. Then I bathed myself in the creek. My dreams and visions had stopped for this moment. I started a fire by the creek that night. I just wanted to rest, enjoy the water and the wonders of the forest around me. I could not take another step; I could not follow the endless meaning of life's suffering anymore. I could not be a witness to the chastisement that happened in the wake of this devalued life.

It was the unborn and the most ancient in me that took me on this journey. The unborn was a mere glimpse of who I am as well as the ancient of me. Time had coupled with physical suffering at every turn on this path. Several signs had come my way from within as an observer of my own corruption and construct. This was so far disastrous to my fragmented self.

Who was the best of us and not one of us? Is there a more suitable person for the task of dismantling me? I have not casted a single word that was in anyway intended to cast away the frailties of life. For the most part, I grew awake in this life, and every one of us had a hand in devaluing death and supporting this estranged waking life.

In the waters and in the wind, I found a promise of sustenance. The trees remained as beacons. In the thick tree lines of the forest, I heard the buzzards at rest and the evening's wind whistling around the herd of them. I gathered rocks, twigs, and sticks to create a fire that night. I could smell a robust rain entering this space that I found sanctuary in.

I looked at the fire that I built, and I saw the small insects curling up to the fire and dancing on the tips of its flames. The sight of this fixated me on my destiny of which I could not see. I thought to myself, I am captivated by the vision and dreams within. It wrapped my heart as a snake curls and coils around its prey. The visions set my soul afire and the dreams were enflamed by a child-like innocence. Every part of my being was corrupted by the very thing that was truly me.

A voice yielded my thoughts that came from the other side of the fire I built. It was the image and voice of a sharply-dressed man. He wore a black suit, a white shirt, a black tie, and black leather dress shoes. Strangely and unbeknownst to me in my waking mind, he casted a bravado that I had never seen before. There was a paralyzing aura about the energy of this figure. It was a two-fold understanding. I did not fear him, yet I remained slightly cautious of this figure. It seemed as if I was the provider of this figure's energy, due to his unyielding focus that he placed on me.

Our souls were not skewed nor blurred in relations. He was no illusion, but truth, and not the truth as told by one's ego. I was him, and he was more of me than I was of him. And therefore, freeing him from the bondage of gratifying me on a mundane level.

The hidden self, bathes in the primordial waters of the soul. Loving yourself is an oxymoron. I had to awaken to the existence of the true essence of love, that which is in slumber in me. Or death would surely catch up with me first, he foretold to me.

Unknown to me, the man in the black suit, that stilled my being, was not to be vexed by me. Nor was I charged with vexing him. But it was my mirrored self who laid next to me in the tower. A shell of my-SELF, the one that could not get up when I arose. This image laid waste, or so I thought, at the bottom of the tower's floor in my dreams and visions.

Traumatized and unaware, I mirrored that image of me, and I was flustered with denial of that fact. However, the man in the suit, this superimposed image of myself, loomed by the fire with me through the night. We were in tune with the movement and crackle of the fire, as well as toned down from our first encounter in my dream within the tower.

The next day I awoke. I had slept through the hard rain, underneath a tree adorned with wide wet leaves and long branches. The hard rain straightened leaves that were before horizontal. With the fire burned out, the twigs and branches were now pieces of smoldering coal. The forest smelled of rain-soaked leaves, water-dampened wood, and fragrant flowers. A few fallen branches laid rest, piled up like driftwood from the heavy rain during the night.

The moist air was not humid nor cool. It seemed to sooth my Being from the abuse of my weathered mind. Making monotone my errant learned ways of life. My breath at that moment was exhilarating. The lukewarm air filled my lungs.

The calmness that I gathered from the aura of the forest was tranquil. I could see nothing through the treetops, except the black birds clinging onto this area, as though in search of a guide or to be a guidepost for me. Leading me to leave, that which was behind me and of present position. Colorful were the black birds' underbellies that mirrored the colors of the forest, from which they flew over.

The birds were not just fowl, but of spirit and it was foolish to follow them. It was as though the birds knew their appointed time and the appointment they had to keep. For every swoop, swoon, and swallow of the birds' flying pattern, it was the dance that the winged ones played, the cycles and patterns in which I had to create, which brought about glimpses of innocence.

I kept going on my journey. With every step, I heard the crunch of the leaves on the forest floor, meshing with grass and the fallen black birds' feathers. Also, the crackling of old limbs of festered trees fallen from yesteryear. What became of my steps was the supplanting of earthly positions and steadfast morals that decayed in this mist of my walk.

I saw a branch, the length of my wingspan, that was neither fractured, splintered, nor rotted. It stood like a rod out of the earth, expanding towards the sky. I gently removed it from its bondage. I looked at it as more than a mere branch; it was a gem in my eyes, now in my grasp.

I also bent over, looking on top of the blades of grass to find a feather; straight, firm, but also flexible. The feather would be incorporated into an arrow I would make one day. Making the arrow stable and precise in flight.

This was a daunting task to look at every feather that I could, that would thus become my arrows fletching. The feather would help carry this spiraled life to my estranged destined soul. I would find out that the mask over my face was nothing more than a mask, concealing the beauty of the dexterity of my love. I have imagined that the flaws and separation of just one feather would send the well struck arrow from my bow awry.

Who would fathom that this smooth feather would pose such a threat to my own desires? Nevertheless, I would be stifled due to the flexibility of the bow that I would first and foremost, create with the branch pulled from the earth. The former, the one arrow, I would create and apply the feather to, would be struck by the bow. This would be the conceived and concealed detriment of the prism that organized my current world. I sat a few yards from where I camped out the previous night, creating my arrow from a small portion of the flesh of this petrified wood branch. I carved the arrow through the bright and vivid day, as well as beyond the evening. It is interesting in the void of light what I could fashion.

If it were not for the blackness of night, my eyes would not glimmer and show the brightness of the dawn of a new day to come. If it were not for the illumination of light, my life would be a grim reminder of the lives born before, without the gift of death to remind me no more. Mere illusions of life and that likeness of me, it is not subject to any one life.

I hope that this arrow that I would make from this seemingly ordinary piece of wood, would one day be the bell of the ball. Was it not for the days, when I was emptied and exhausted of mind and of things that love propped me up? As does a stick, much like the one I wrestled out of the forest floor, does for a dilapidated wall.

For most of the night, I carved my arrow with a jagged sharp rock. The bow which after spending some time on, resembled a slightly curved walking stick. In the mid of the night, palms course and rough, fingertips slightly bruised and splintered. The wet and damp night before had dried away. I gathered all my things and began back on my journey through the rest of the night. I could hear the nocturnal creatures awaken with howls, screeching, and cat calls.

As dawn approached, the black birds were still hovering. I heard from a distance the wondering footsteps of someone or something. I saw within the forest a young boy playing. He played with the ever-present awareness of himself, without fear, that which would seemingly make one enriched with pride. The young boy seemed to marvel in play at the creation of his own playful intelligence. He was one with all that surrounded him. There was an oath made with the boy and the forest. I kept walking towards him, and then I began to circle his area of play in the forest, so that I would not disturb him.

As I approached him, the boy did not hear one step of mine, nor any brush being moved. I placed my hand upon his shoulder. He turned his head around quickly, not surprised, startled, or even wondering why I was there.

I asked the young boy, "What are you doing here and where are you from?"

"From a place where the mountains rest upon the valley," he replied. He proceeded to be unaware of where to go. "I am lost. I seemed to have wondered into the forest that is not of us."

I questioned, "Not of us?" He just gazed and said, "Not of us, but of our spirits."

I took it upon myself to help him find his home. "What is your name?" I asked.

"I have no name. I am of the mountain. I am called upon and I come to its call. But now I cannot hear its call." There was no reply that would be fitting for me to question.

I just looked at him with a veil of self-assured eyes and a half smile. "How about I call you Boy?" The boy shrugged his shoulders, as though he was simply happy to be in the company of someone who he thought was lost as well. He also looked at me with a sense of awe and relief.

For it was just a moment ago that he gazed at the forest and played in the forest shadows with not a care or worry. He asked me of my name, and I replied, "I am The Traveller in this land."

"Where is your home?" he asked.

"I seek my home, but it remains in the land of places that no longer exist as they once were."

The child smelled of sulfur and salt. His clothes had pieces of the black bird's feathers stuck in it. The fallen pieces of leaves were incrusted into his clothing as well. In his eyes, I could see the people of that mountain. The people he spoke of who were of the mountain that sat in the valley. I knew of this child and the people of this place, just as an idea of his; an illusion that I wanted to know, just for comfort for the moment.

I pointed in a direction to which we should go. The boy walked in front of me. I figured he would hear the call, whatever that was. As we began to traverse through the forest, I could see no end, but we continued as though the call would be near. I hoped he would hear the call soon. The boy asked me if I liked stories. I replied, "Yes, as much as anyone, I suppose." I figured we could pass time and forget about being unaware of finding our destination.

He told me that the night before, he wondered into the forest, that two women came to him in a dream. The dream took place in a room that had shear curtains from ceiling to floor. He spoke of beautiful white sheer gleaming curtains. They filled the room, hanging in a maze-like pattern. The boy stated that he tried to find his way through the room. The two women that came to him had given him a clock's hand in the room of this dream. By the time he awoke, he was in the forest. They led him away from his home, away from the mountain and his people.

I envisioned the placement of the clock's hand in this boy's hand. As a place where so little time was given. Yet, all of eternity was given to him through the two women that he had mentioned. He told me he said thank you to the two women for leading him astray, for which he did not know why. He thanked them anyway. The reason for which they came and had given him the clock's hand, I perceived it as a passing of the torch to the boy. A royal ceremony had happened in his dream, although it was merely a clock's hand, they had given him in the dream.

We walked throughout the day on our path. With the black birds overhead, circling us and moving as we moved. And without this call ever coming, we came upon the edge of the forest, opening itself to a lush green valley. I saw a people unconcerned with this valley, let alone us walking through it.

I saw their homes affixed on the exterior surface of the mountain. As my last step left the forest, I felt the core of this mountain's breath brush upon me. The piping of the sulfated air spewed forth madly throughout the valley. Even the black birds of the forest paused at the edge, where the forest met the valley. It was the suspension of their flight path coordinating with our movement.

The forest seemed to sift us both out, purging us from its domain. The forest was not in Love with humanity or its plaguing of souls, but I lived in humanities arc. Abhorred by the pressing of my own skin against my Astro-body.

As we walked closer to the mountain and the people who dwelled there, I began to see the cracks in the mountain's landscape. What was I giving up to be here? To engage with them, could possibly be in grave error. From the time I left my home weeks had gone by on this journey... possibly months. I just wanted to be unseen, one who was rumored to be a spook and never to be spoken of.

As we moved through the green valley, I saw a woman who paused in her act of gathering rocks from the mountain. She paused, as if awakened or startled by something, forgetful of her present task. She saw the boy walking with me through the valley. She dropped her basket of rocks and ran towards us, meeting us at the cusp, where the valley meets the base of the mountain.

She was a motherly figure of course. And while connecting with the boy, I could see the undoing of her worry and sorrow. I could see the pardon and peace that would divorce her present anguish. They all began to file in and fill out at the base of the mountain, as there was a stoppage in their revered routine of work, I suppose. The well-adorned leader amongst them spoke to the boy, ridiculing him for being lost in the forest, in which, it seemed they feared. The leader turned to me, staring into my eyes, but never seeing my soul.

"Which of these stones can we give you of lavish and adorned loot, for returning this boy back to us?"

"I have been given which, has no stone attached to it," I replied. The mother of this boy examined him and held on to him, not as if he were hurt, but as if he were taken. The crowds of people looked and judged the boy, while expressing shame and ridiculing him as well. His eyes were as the forest. I could see the black birds that once accompanied us, swirling in his mind freely.

In an instant, I noticed they all needed each other. Bread of ignorance, with the pointing of their fingers and the wagging of their tongues. They tacked the boy's flesh to this mountain with their heartless welcoming. For not even the thick skinned of them could resist wearing the skin of him. For the fact that he had lost himself and gained the forest's perspective, they were turned off by this; his renewed and found spirit.

Those of this mountain could not even breathe without their ever-present hammers and pickaxes at their very fingertips; they all carried them. There was a dimness over the land. Dimmer than the caves and caverns in which they worked. The light of fainted torches and the will of an ignorant heart. There is nothing forever in this environment. In the midst of taking away the heart of the boy's venture, they introduced and induced their minds with erroneous and untruthful propaganda about the boy's time away.

The mother hugged the boy, but not to bestow too much compassion or relief to him. In her eyes, I saw what she had to place above the boy, and it was the belief of the masses. I saw a familiar disease that existed in them. In my former ways and even currently, I even saw the angels that they had not seen. I had to evolve from evoking those aloof and aloft perpetrators. This evolution was such a masochism of pain and pleasurable moments.

Their own hearts were beaten into the cold and heartened stones. The masses of them, their faces were erased of compassion. Their denial was not to be free of their own judgments. And now the leader spoke to them implying that there is a beast that lives in the boy's heart. Every one of them encircled the boy. Cupping their hands, then pouring the warm spring waters that leaked from the mountainside over his head and body. The mountain was their supple mother, cleansing the boy of his troubled travels.

I returned the boy to his mother. Not for her sake, but for the sake of an anticipated truce. The truce for which I could tell could be the death to all or one of them. This would be a sacrifice to upkeep the mountain's symbolic majesty that had plagued them all beyond reproach.

The leader amongst them told me that I could rest for a time. In respect of the fact, that I returned the boy, he stated, "You may rest for a few days, then you can choose to stay and be one with us or be gone from here."

"Thank you," I replied, as I glanced at the enormous girth of the mountain, now being the only thing, I saw from the inner canthus of my eye to the outer canthus. The mountain stood almost immortal over the valley, but not even its shadow entered the valley.

The mother of the boy, from what I could understand, her compassion and Love were not to be placed over the masses. All of them had lost their hearts and their heads. At the base of the mountain, the masses of them began to clear out, as they had work to be done. The boy's mother grabbed my hand, and with her touch, she grabbed my spirit as well. We parted with the residents of this place and started on our way, scaling, and walking upon the face of the mountain where her home was.

We approached her home, and she softly pushed against the door that was made of mud, gravel, gems, wood, and stones. These things were unearthed some time ago, as the door looked fossilized with the things that were structurally incased in it. There was a release of heaviness from the boy's mother as we entered her home. With the slightest touch again, she closed the door behind us. She found herself no longer longing or concealed by the idealized thoughts of the masses.

She stated that her home was adorned with the things that were found deep within the mountain's caverns. The mud, gravel, gems, and stones also aligned the interior walls of the home. The light from the candles revealed the gems incrusted in the walls of the dwelling as well. I could smell her spirit in this home. She was moved by my wondering eyes. As though she had never seen anyone that was a traveler from afar. Not many words were spoken.

I ate with her, and the boy returned from the hordes of people washing him and brainwashing him. I noticed his demure demeanor as he entered the home later.

As night gathered, the stars and the arcs of comets were in the sky. The boy and his mother cuddled in their bed. They sunk in the center of their bed as they slept, holding one another. I found myself lying on the floor in the adjacent room inside her home, on a makeshift pallet, gazing at the luminary stones and gems in the ceiling before falling asleep.

Not long after falling asleep, there I was again, sitting with Robyn, the woman with red hair. This time she looked at me as though I was more than just a friend. The train that we were on previously, we were on again. I could see out the window of the train cart. In the distance, I saw a flood of water coming from every direction to the bank of the railroad track.

The embankment against the train track protected us from the flood waters. The train's path was going directly forward, somewhere that I did not know. We moved along this path with a buzzing of iron against iron. It loosened the chain of bridled Love. It made everything, and every thought, complete in Love. And it was in this dream and not from anything gained from the degenerate known world. The Love that I felt in Robyn's presence ejected the ego without falsely identifying Love's position.

It seemed like a complete debauchery. But it was a grand orgy of Epicurious delight. I could see my steadfast ignorance of so-called spiritual ideologies shook, quivering and shivering abandoning me. The past ideologies attempting to castrate this beautiful, endearing feeling of the sexuality of the soul within me, before its fatal jump from my spirit.

I was experiencing the fullness of the soul through this intimacy. The embodiment of the provocative bow was always being fashioned. It was the most holy alter, the most holy temple. I carved away at the arrow from deep within my mind. My physical being was the bow's bones, spine, and mass.

This erotic friendship of love had impregnated us with a beautiful courtship. This beautiful courtship was indescribable. But best described as the love of friendship that is Philia, a divine friendship of Love. I gathered this was the place of her origins.

That night as I fashioned my arrow, Robyn also helped me to create a smoother shaft for my bow, that would calm my being and physical body. That way, in my periods of rest in my travels, I could precisely and in patience, possibly produce the perfect bow. Also, she forged and introduced me to a sword that I would ultimately use to cut myself. With this sword I would cut my-SELF in half and be one with her.

It was a precise and erect cutting from my head to the lower parts of thought and physicality. I had to hide it in my dreams so that my moral thoughts and my mental conditioning would not dull the blade.

My mental attitude toward this rich envisioned environment, was the rust that could react to this precious element of love between me and Robyn. The oxygen taken in by one's words, the hydrogen expelled by one's intentions, and the electrical current that plagued human interaction. Even the earth that I walked upon in my waking life was filled with the bacteria that ate away at our mystical innards. Hiding the gem of a Soul.

In remembrance, I laid down not my bow or my arrow, but I laid down the formidable act of knowing. My divine spirit and soul striking the veil of time, ignorance, and those aspired intellects of truths, that were all but one untruth.

That morning, I awakened to the seeping light that caused a glittering effect into the home. I ate of slow-cooked rabbit and greens and drank of the cooled spring waters from the mountains' landscape. The woman and I walked through the passages and the core of the mountain.

In the act of extracting resources from this mountain, the people labored throughout the day and night. I rubbed my hands along the walls of the caves that ran throughout the mountain. I could feel the trauma and the traumatic institutional ideas that so carefully seeded the minds of them. She asked, "How did you come across my son? Where did you come from?" Her child told her that I presented myself as the Traveller.

I spoke and told her…

"The forest in which I found your son lost in, while playing with the likes of his innocents, his childish and whimsical reality was uninhibited. He seemed to have no barrier to his uninfluenced thought. I am The Traveller in this land. I come from a place that remains in the land of places that no longer exist as they once were."

She seemed unconcerned to ask any more questions about my past whereabouts. However, it pleased her heart to know of places beyond this land. It was all like a fantasy to her, not a real place. Her reality was this town that cast the shadow of the mountain upon the valley, but never did their physical bodies cast a shadow upon the forest. For the forest was but its own justifiable suffering system, unlike this land's system of unjust and agreed imprisonment.

I was there, with her, in the mountain. I had taken a liking to her. She was of my dreams and a part of my fragmented soul. The pinnacle of my soul's Love; she was not. The essence of her drew a piece of the puzzling path to my Ultimate Love.

She told me of her fondness to please the elders and to stay true to the Gods of the Mountain. "The stones and gems bring us life. We see inspiration and hope in our acts of mining this mountain. You would be pleased to know, Traveler, and it would please far more than your spirit, to gratify our Gods and elders. They are our truth. And as told to us, came to this mountain before us.

It is our paradise that you see as this mountain. Our rich history, our protection, and our peace." As we walked, she noticed me gazing at the tedious and insufferable work of them all. Everyone was involved in the extraction. She asked, "Can you see this love for our mountain, in our work?"

I see love as one seamless purpose and one that needs no guide or aggressive pursuit. You are the Being that you wait for and the Being that you should serve. You are the rare gem that you have not yet found in this mountain.

Your ancestors, I do not know of. Though the Love that is here is a remnant of something that has gone by. It appears you are all trying to catch the past, which has little to no power. I live with Love as my confidant and my aim. My breath is infinite; it is but a wave of essences of past, present, and future lives. Giving life within, to my soul.

She asked, "Why do you speak of our God, as if you, are disgruntled with our Deity?"

"When I set my soul free, I began to take many forms," I replied. "For my ascension keeps me trapped in a realm, not so different than how you labor in this mountain. To omit the things of ungracefulness along with upholding my gracefulness is the fault of a demoralized mind. I count all as goodness, and for me to see the two and know it is One, allows me to open the veins of my Soul. Lubricating those veins with the serum of death. Hopefully, thereafter, I will be sunken into the sound of my true soul's heartbeat, if only for a moment."

I foreshadowed love, just by the mere fact of being here with her in this mountain. I was all but lost in the caverns of this mountain. Then our peace was interrupted by the picking, scraping, and carving at the guts of the mountain's core, at a passageway leading outside the mountain.

I saw the hammers, sickles, and picks that day, ruining their spirit. Under the wrath of the sun and the cold of the evening. They set their sights on the gems and missed the gem that mirrored their heart-centered thoughts. From years of neglect, they created clots and stoppage of flow from their ideologies that clogged their hearts.

I was a very solid form of my former human self. The very awareness of my soul brought upon a sort of finality. I picked and scraped as well, to unearth my soul. The gems of the mountain were like the remnants of my former self. A life of trinkets and trash pushed upon the shore of my mobile suffering.

The thirsty sun began to sip from the large dipping cup and set upon the horizon. As I talked with the boy's mother, I was approached in mid-conversation by the leader of the people. He said to me, "Have you decided to remain with us or leave?"

"I believe my rest has been adequate for the return to my travels," I replied. "I appreciate the time you have given me. For my mind and my feet have been given rest."

He then spoke to the boy's mother. "Can you leave us for a moment, my dear?"

"Yes, my leader," she replied. She then stated to me, "I will make a meal for you that will fill you well beyond your morning's journey." She then walked away towards her home to prepare such a meal.

The leader asked me, "Traveler, where are you off to? Back to the forest, I presume?"

"I have no destination. However, I know my direction will not take me from which I came. So, if you are asking if I will return to the forest…The forest will always be with me, in my travels. Although, it is but one column in the spine of my path."

He then said, as he cut me off from finishing my words, "What are you, some sort of Messenger?"

I spoke with the intent to cause no confusion and to be precise in my words. "Who envies the messenger of oneself? I have had infinite amounts of messengers who have come to me and others. And when they came, they brought a fool's gold of hope. Heaped upon the curvature of the minds who were lost. It was a dim world for us all back then, before the start of my journey."

"Whosoever envies a messenger, who must go within the darkness of oneself to unveil the darkness and the whole light of your true self? Who envies the messenger that realizes the honorable and divine You? And whom of the Messengers comes only to others as a selfless Angel, not to save anyone? Love saves, if you but only knew. I shall BE a messenger, not of ALL, but unto All of ME. There is a plethora of messengers who have plagued and calcified the entrance of the doorway to the soul. Though I am but one soul. I salivate at the taste of salvation from this sweet soul."

The leader of the town had witnessed the superimposed image of myself that evening. He looked upon me as a tyrant. However, I was the tyrant of his idols. Their idols were jealous ones and did not care for the erotic life of the soul's outpour. Their god was brutal in its approach to anyone picking at their flesh for one's soul.

Time and I were not the same anymore…But the linear lines of a lucid concept of time that I once indulged in with grimace and gratefulness changed me. Truth be told, I watched nature and the populous slaughter themselves in coexistence, and it aroused me.

The heavens would not agree, and a pretentious God was determined to do away with me. This God created nothing in the minds of people, but the thoughts and actions of a passive mule.

He told me that he could see why and how I found the boy. I could not see it at the time in its totality, but he gave a description of the boy's character.

"That boy that you brought back to us should have remained gone. The town now talks of the forest as a vestige, instead of being vexed. You see the boy would not work in the mountain as the rest of the children. The rest of them mimicked every movement and thought of the elders, in hopes to one day be a part of the great historical works of our undertaking. Instead, this boy toiled in the valley, at every chance he could find. I would observe him at the edge of the valley right before the entrance to the forest, speaking unto the forest.

The boy says it is a dream that led him into the forest, as though he sleepwalks with the evil spirits of the forest. The boy was better off dead in the wilds of the forest lure. Our elders spoke not to go near it. For the forest would bring misfortune for all of us, if entered by just one of us. I would have cut the throat of this boy, if it were not for his mother, who has unearthed many of our most precious stones and gems. The boy has always been indifferent to our ways. I have observed this since he could speak and crawl."

"Where is the boy?" I asked the leader.

"Doing the work of works in the mountain," he replied. "As he should be, deep within the mountain. He shall work through the night and get more accustomed to this life."

The leader of them then turned away from me, staring at the mountain's entrance. I asked him, "Why is it that you all crave for the acceptance of your idol's Love, from a gem or a stone? You are deprived from the wonders of the stars. If you would look up and stop bowing to a rock."

He turned his head and asked, "Can you see your works in the stars?" He was drunk in his own worship.

"It is the light of the stars that gives projection to this world," I replied. "Yet, you dwell in the pits of the dim mountain. What is your hope in mining the caves of this mountain?"

"There is no hope in mining the caves of the mountain. We feed our spirit and provide inspiration to the lesser and greater of us. This mountain is our very life; that is the prophesy for the people of this mountain.

"And if you do not mine the mountain?" I replied.

"Then we shall be deepened in the soot that fills the air and walls of the mountain. And that shall mean the end of us."

"Maybe that is what shall be and what might be best," I proposed.

The leader spoke in an authoritative voice. "You speak of death as though it is life. Death is but a crux, and you shall be eager to walk into the urge of the light again after this life. And my idol as you call our great god, shall meet you at that passage point of light for reentry."

"This light you speak of, is served on a smudged plate, as result of your human appetite. And you dine in a prison world, where all are free to ignore the walls that surround them like a coffin."

"Goodnight, Traveler. May you rest well for your journey in the morning." I parted from the leader. Waiting to see the truth and falseness that lied upon this plane of earth. Hoping before I left this mountain, I would see the light in each crevice of this cavernous mountain swelling and irritating its underbelly.

The moonlight in the night's darkness lit the walkway. As I scaled up that path to the home of the boy's mother, I thought, why did I descend upon this mountain? I could have let the boy go at the edge of the forest. My mind digested my thoughts of the day. We were all wrapped in this lie of generalizing the ways of each other's minds. The mystery remained ... why was there such a divide?

That night in her home, I was struck with the uncontrollable desire of a grave digger's preserving of a Soul. Her soul had been preserved in the container of this terrestrial lifestyle. It is this terrestrial lifestyle that enhanced the flavor profile of her spirit.

She knew this meal she prepared for me was a meal to be tasted, drank, and eaten. Not only of the fowl, vegetation, and the fruitful wine; but also, to taste of her rich olive tone skin. Which with every sumptuous kiss, had a different taste profile upon my lips. On this night, with the attractive mixing of spirits, she gave purpose to her statement of me being full, well beyond my morning's journey.

She held, kissed, and looked at the veins in my hand, which pulsated to the beat of my heart. The gift she gave to me was from a resonating echo of love trying to overcome her hidden pain. We opened each other's hearts to find treasures. The reclusive ways of our own piety vanished. The escapism into this sensual spiritual world was through our touch and intercourse.

She was delicate, and I proposed to my own soul, not to break and disrupt her delicate being. It was not for me to nurture, but rather for us to be pruned. I kissed her, as though I was trying to open a door within me. We sought each other, only to find ourselves trying to never to be sought by each other again.

We were fragmented lovers, and never the lovers that we ultimately would find. Nevertheless, she took refuge in our kiss and the stirring of our hearts. We were the pain and suffering of one's life eclipsing. Setting the stage someday within ourselves to depart from our own reflection. She exhausted herself that night and would always be remembered by me. But not the one of my dreams; she was not the one for me. Though she was more real to me than the mountain they revered. But not real enough for me.

I could never claim her as day to my night. We could never be lovers at the twilight. We were not for one another, and yet we were connected to each other's paths. I asked her, "Can you see Love beyond your hindsight? It forms within. I know this to be true."

"How can I believe?" she asked.

"For the wind is formidable enough," I replied. "The object of its affection is the waters; this causes the wind to be aware of itself. Realizing this, strengthens the waves of water and gusts of winds, to be at peace and the object of one's desires."

I made love to her like the winds whirl around an object. A wind that allows you not to catch your breath when face to face with it. I was caressed by her restless lower form of love and it awakened my sense of being.

Afterwards, she presented to me, while we laid in bed, an unpolished black stone. In fact, it was a black diamond, with coal and ore still surrounding most of its surface. There was a precise and evident reason why she gave me this imperfect stone. She opened her hand and placed the unpolished black diamond within mine. Although unpolished, the mountain had yielded to her this stone, this rock, that represented her current imperfection and authenticity.

I thought its only viable use was to forge an arrowhead. I would file its exterior, so one day, it would be used to pierce this hardened world.

My desires fleeting as the sheets of the bed swayed from the gentle breeze that came into her home. This breeze seemed to caress and admire our display of love. I cradled her in my arms while she rested. Her love was like this stone she had given me.

The center of her heart dazzled with the light of love, trying to break free from the encasement of life. Not knowing that the rusted and dull pickaxe of her will could strike at this world's flawed charm, chucking this brittle encasement away from her heart.

The breeze that night turned into the pouring down of rain and storm gusts. You could feel the thunder and lightning rocking the mountain. We were concealed and calmed by the sound. Her home was filled with the heat of hedonism and a pleasurable peace.

"You shall leave here in the morning," she said. "But I wish to know that you will think of me. In moments I cannot visualize and in places that I cannot see. I ask that you govern yourself as though everyone and everything is precious. I can tell that you realized, thus far in your journey, that the satisfaction you sought in your old world was propaganda. That is why you only need protection from yourself."

We slept as lovers waiting for the morning light to come between us and separate our bodies.

At daybreak, an abrupt and forceful knock at the door broke our sleep. The mother of the boy grabbed her clothing and rushed to clothe herself before opening the door. It was an elder woman of the mountain at the door. The elder woman shouted, "The boy, the boy!"

"What is going on?" the boy's mother asked.

The older woman shouted franticly, "The boy has fallen into the mountain's core!" Before she could finish those words, the boy's mother rushed to the mountain. She saw people gathered around the entrance.

She walked in the center of the crowd that was gathered there. She saw him lying there with his eyes, chest, and arms seemingly bleeding with the dark oils of the mountain's secretion. He had ventured into the mountain's core that night. He had the black bird's feathers in hand that he had picked from the forest.

He had thrown the black feathers into the steamy swells of the mountain's inner springs. In which the boiling hot waters mixed with the feathers and the soot of the mountain. It produced this dark black brood that ran from every orifice of the mountain.

His mother shouted, "You promised me you would work, and still your curiosity and innocence for me."

The leader shouted to the masses, "He is but a boy who toiled in the mountain and lost his footing."

It was a great lie that cloaked itself to be true. Unknowing and knowingly, this was the backbone of the prophesy that the leader of them feared.

It was a great lie that cloaked itself to be true. Unknowing and knowingly, this was the backbone of the prophesy that the leader of them feared.

The sheer pouring of this complete mystical brew stained the boy's body. It was a great vision and an act of beauty. This mountain did not know the divine sensual opening that it unveiled at the crux of the boy's heart. The creosote was vivacious in its nature. I knew of this bathing of the body. It has a cold grasp that warms your Being.

I was in the presence as an observer. Observing the persona of his mother's selflessness and protection. Her son's eyes displayed a chaotic beauty. He would always be hers in moral and mental fabric. He was once ripped from her flesh. She would always remember the scars of that moment. But the scar of knowing he was with her in any capacity was better than losing him in this world. Her past and the pressure from her peers had built this so-called holy place in her mind. However, her aura and light were dimmed by this world.

Creation in the eyes of those who stood around the boy was finite. Their creator was the promising potter, from which the clay, mud, and dirt of this unseen creator fashioned it all. They claimed origins that were kept on a balance sheet. Showing what their God had given them and what they owed with their spiritual annexation. Their erroneous origins made them have a sense of belonging.

The people of the mountain turned over on all fours and began to salivate at the idea of ostracizing the boy. I saw the boy as me. Who could not be seen by the eyes of the people of this mountain? Coiled minds could not uncoil and straighten. The broadness of the spiritual flesh had to shed the crust from their eyes for the soul to gain its fullness.

Their minds, once flooded with anger, were now flushed with the idea that the boy was not of them anymore. His mother knew it. He thanked her for being his mother with his actions. He stood upright on his feet and took a tight grasp of her hand. They then began to walk through the valley. Now somewhat of marshland from the overflow of the soot like water running from every vein of the mountain.

The people watched the boy and his mother walk across the valley, closer and closer towards the forest. With a fledgling breeze that cooled their weighted necks, with their gems and stones adorned around them, they all stood and stared from the mountain at the boy and his mother.

My eyes scanned towards the darkness of this cave. I saw things of myself just yesterday in the bowels of the mountain. The people of this land were broad sighted, with no foresight. All of us were intertwined in a sequence of events that meant absolutely nothing.

The depths of the illicit nominal ignorance that dripped away to get to this point, just to swallow whole the truth of a dying world, piercing a dying age. In the caverns of this mountain, with its squealing winds, from its lowest points, I wanted to know how to piece myself together, from the severed and unenjoyed parts of my-SELF.

So, as the boy and his mother walked to the end of the valley approaching the forest entrance, I said goodbye to her within my head. I had gained more of her restless love than her soul. We never were brilliant in this world. We were of unknown origins that originated beyond the force of the stars that this mountain sat under. They entered the forest as the seekers of lands not inhabited by them. What was this ever-descending methodology of placing earthly origins upon ourselves?

There were too many facets of this life that were marred with embellishments of the truth. This embellishment had no weight in Love. This is what thrusted me into that forest to begin with. I now live in a place that has no ending and no beginning.

I gained the petrified wood from the forest to be my eventual bow someday. But currently, I use it as a staff to stay steady on my path. The staff with origins, merely of a spiritual seed and a mortal tree. The tree from which this staff comes from was already hardened by the stringent and stagnate air of this earth's realm. These were my thoughts as the boy played with his mother with gratefulness. The boy garnered his mother's hair with a black feather that had fallen from the black birds to the forest floor.

The people of the mountain watched in contempt. They saw the spirit of the boy completely losing its' covering, being unraveled by the forest. The hoard of them stood in anger, as though they wanted to hurl the rocks that they clinched in their hands at the boy.

His mother watched him play as the whimsical fool. He was just as I had found him in the forest days ago. Those who stood here on the mountain, held back their tears like a dilapidated dam. With a range of emotions, from rage to disgust and pain. The innate tolerance from the jagged stones and sharp gems they mined for a lineage, was pleasurable inside their scarred and bloody hands.

"So, what shall we do?" they all asked the leader of the mountain.

"The prophecy said we would be taken by the soot, but the boy was just an accident. He is not a sign from our Gods." A few of them glanced again at the boy and his mother. The boy grabbed an armful of feathers from the forest floor and playfully threw them into the lush green valley.

At that moment, a handful of them left from the side of the mountain. They decided to participate in whatever the boy and his mother were doing. They rushed towards the forest to gather feathers in the day...that is what they did on this day.

All the stones that were in the baskets and hands of the handful who left, laid waste upon the side of the mountain. It was the stones that they took so many years to mine and polish. The few of them who walked away from this life of the mountain, would mean there might be many who would one day walk away, and have understanding someday.

The boy's foolish approach to life brought a pouring of love over those who left the mountain. His foolish act became law to those few. A spark of this love creates, albeit, a glimpse of the destruction, of not only this mountain but an entire world, and I was an eyewitness to this destruction.

They were at a problematic point on the axis of the entire universe. In their partiality, it was an apparent loss of this mountain's scape, its' inhabitants, the Gods that dwelled here, and the farce of a prophecy. But it was apparent that this could be ruined by even a child's mind.

The leader amongst them looked at me with a sterile vengeance. He walked towards me, standing face to face with me. "All of you, pick up your tools and let us work harder than ever before. This is for our God's will and promises. So, that the least of us will never be blindsided by the will of a fool or a foolish boy. And you, sir, The Traveller, as you call yourself; you shall part from us, and never walk upon this mountain or land again. If you do, you will not be met next time with such open arms!"

I told him, and all of them who stood there with him, "There will be a day that the stones of the mountain will be lighter than your spiritual text, laws, and your servitude."

I then stated, "To walk upon your lands, with you and your God again, would mean I have become as an orphan to my Soul. It would mean that the fire that burned in me is now a mere candle that has burned out. Creating a wax disfigurement of my true self. It shall mean that the war that rages in me has produced an infant again, and I once more, must suckle from ignorance.

So, if you see me again, have a blade made of this world ready for me. To cut the throat of that infant. Because if you do not, I might be as the boy, and cut the throat of your God with the straight edge of my bow's arrow that carries upon my Soul's Love."

"You shall leave now, Traveller," he said in a tempered rage.

We parted ways by the entrance of the mountain. The leader was vexed by his own moralistic ways. He walked into the mountain, deep into its core, and wiped himself with the creosote from its walls, taking the prophecy away from the boy. This meant nothing. He wiped his face, chest, and entire body, trying to look like the boy. The image of the innocence of the boy could not be replicated by someone so repulsed by it.

I grabbed my things, my staff, my unfinished arrow, and the unpolished black diamond stone. I wrapped and tucked these items within my shirt covering.

As I was leaving this mountain, I wandered to the side of the mountain range. Seeing the masses of them going into the mountain to do what they always do… mine. And the continued gathering of feathers from the forest by the boy, his mother, and the few of them.

In the distance, I could see their war approaching, as though a cloud had been ushered away revealing the light of those few who left the mountain. The light of the few disturbed the thoughts of those who stayed on this mountain…at work.

The few of them who were in the valley, their infinite souls had cracked its mummified state. They had grown above the heights of the mountain from which they had just turned away. They saw the black birds as themselves. The whole of nature, in their nature.

Those in the forest gathering were now experiencing their sweat-filled garments encountering the fresh spring-like air of the forest. The forest air blew the cool air over their cuts and blisters. Their hands laid soaked with blood spilling onto the earth from their years of torment in the mountain. For they had mined day and night under the guise of perfecting that which could not be perfected.

Would they evolve enough to make the seeds of their own suffering rot in peril? They only released their folly, but it took time to recant the rite. Error was all they knew. They wronged themselves from outward in. They had tarnished the gem at the knob of the spine. I hoped they would never confuse radical with radiant, nor collaborator with consciousness.

In the years to come, I would have visions of the mountain. The physical wars, the tribulations of the fractured groups of them. They still longed to hear from their God, who sat idly. This God feeds from the blunt force of intercession and devotion of the masses. After a while, the boy would never be seen again by anyone, not even his mother. He would enter that forest and lose himself.

The few of them would struggle in that valley that they made a home. Stuck between two worlds. One being her son's innocence of heart, free of the diet of their deity. And secondly, her regret of the years of living on the face of that mountain. In the valley, she was cattle to the people living on the mountain. Her and the few of them, would have to flee or fight those of the mountain. They had no aptitude of reasoning and could not be reasoned with. Their so-called mountain of a God wanted to con and crown only a gullible spirit. And the leader of those in the mountain had this suitable characteristic.

I left behind the overcoat of divinity at the swell of the mountain's passing; in thought, in intimacy, and in the deliverance of my own self-worth. Open as a blooming flower, letting the rays strike its light upon every facet of my pallet. Without the façade of trying to be of mortal man to get by.

I was miles away from them now. Far in footsteps, and numerous imprints of my feet indented into many terrains left behind.

I carried nothing of them but the boy's foolish appetite to know and the unpolished stone. It was a rough and uncut black diamond, unacquainted with its' natural beauty, like the woman whom it was given by.

I came to a passageway. The landscape was abundant with purple flowers. The flowers swayed slowly, almost rhythmically from the gentle wind. The purple flowers placed my mind at ease.

I could not fathom the fairness of the illusion of this world, when the reality of this woman appeared amongst me in this broad, purple flower-filled passageway. She came to me with hair as black as the depths of the universe, skin so beautiful, a rich blackened mahogany color. It was as though she was me, and I was her finite essence.

I understood that she was the appearance of all that appears factual to me. I stood there looking upon the rich purple flowers everywhere around me. The appearance of her seemed to be of a much older version of my soul. A time and place that was so distant from my waking mind.

This being, this woman, softly grabbed my face, caressing and grasping my facial cheeks, as a mother would. I felt this energy of her as a destroyer and an originator. She would have had, on any other day, destroyed the purple field, the passageway, land and earth, as well as the endless abyss included ... If I had only known of my Self then.

She was my darkness, the "so be it" and "the means." She was my mother, who hated the wet nursing of a mortal, but understood the discipline it took to slice a ray of light. She knew that a mortal could raise her son to the height of the dark abyss. I felt her stare at the side of my face, as though she missed my presence in her womb and in her arms. I stood still in the luminescence of the purple fields.

She spoke into my ear and said ...

www.ingramcontent.com/pod-product-compliance
Lightning Source LLC
Chambersburg PA
CBHW020604130626
46552CB00007B/3034